Wild Spaces

WILD SPACES

S. L. CONEY

TOR PUBLISHING GROUP

NEW YORK

WILD SPACES

Cover design by FORT

A Tordotcom Book
Published by Tom Doherty Associates / Tor Publishing Group
120 Broadway
New York, NY 10271

www.tor.com

Tor® is a registered trademark of Macmillan Publishing Group, LLC.

ISBN 978-1-250-86684-4 (ebook)
ISBN 978-1-250-86683-7 (trade paperback)

First Edition: 2023

For Ishy, the very best good boy

Wild Spaces

I

The dog shows up at the mint-green house on the edge of the woods a month before the monster arrives, his coat shiny as a new copper penny. Right away, the boy knows he's special, even though his mother says all dogs make you feel that way. She stands back, an arm crossed over her chest, chewing a thumbnail as she watches the boy and his father both kneeling in the grass of the front yard, petting the animal. He runs his fingers through the dog's long fur and rubs his soft ears, the shape and size of him reminding the boy of a friend's golden retriever. The dog's tail beats the ground as he pants and smiles, eyes half-closed like this is the most blissful thing ever.

"He probably belongs to someone," she says, speaking around the tip of her thumb.

"He doesn't have a collar," his father says, "and he's pretty skinny." He leaves the boy and dog in the grass and wraps his arms around his wife from behind, hugging her close. "You're eating your nail polish again." His father begins swaying side to side just a little, murmuring into her hair, and his mother shrugs. He smirks and walks two fingers up her arm. She catches his hand before he can tickle her and turns her head, trying not to smile.

"We'll put an ad in the paper," his father says.

They wait a week, then two. But no one claims the dog, and finally his mother acquiesces. They name him Teach—after the boy's favorite pirate—because his father says they can't call him Blackbeard on account of his red fur, and those weeks before life upends are nearly perfect.

The boy and Teach spend early summer evenings playing baseball in the field by the waterway—the boy always playing third base just like his dad on the Charleston RiverDogs—and being pirates down by the cave on the beach, burying treasure and avoiding the dark where they're not allowed.

At home, they lie stretched underneath the table, the smell of chicken and pineapple wafting from the oven. His father and mother dance around the kitchen to Glenn Miller on his father's record player. His mother smiles open-mouthed, lips scarlet red, her curling hair black and shiny. His father, slim and angular with a cleft in his chin and bright, intelligent eyes, brushes his hand over her back as he crosses behind her, resting it on her shoulder as he stirs one of the pots and she slices the bread. They're movie stars in black and white, a full-orchestra-in-the-background kind of pretty.

At night, the boy's mother tucks him into bed beneath the Jolly Roger hanging on his wall. He can smell Ivory soap on her hands—crisp and clean as she smooths the covers around him. She tells him she's writing a new book, about the pirate Madame Cheng, and he pictures his mother leading the Red Flag Fleet against the Portuguese, refusing to stand down.

And in the night, before they sleep, he presses his lips to Teach's silken ear and tells him secrets—like the bottle rocket hidden under his bed—knowing they're safe. And Teach, sometimes, tells him some back.

———————

When the boy's grandfather rolls down the gravel drive in the station wagon, its wooden side panels rattling, he brings something with him. It's in his mother's odd, closed-mouth smile and his father's confused glances. It's in the shaking under his fingers when Teach growls at the man who climbs out of the car.

The family leaves the porch with the hollow *thwack* of wood against wood, the screen door bouncing shut behind them. In the gray area between the electric light at the edge of the house and the dark of night, the raccoon sneaking into the outdoor shower retreats, back hunched as he runs.

The old man stands, tall and barrel-chested, his shoulders straight and strong, his unlined face topped by a shiny bald head. He looks less like a grandfather and more like the man on the bottle of cleaner the boy's mother uses to mop the floor. But the old man's eyes, those are unmistakable—they're the same deep, turbulent blue as his mother's, as his own.

They stand in an uneven huddle, the cicadas' song swelling around them as the insects devour their way down the coast.

It's the old man's shoes that catch the boy's attention. The black dress shoes are caked with sand, their hard edges digging into the naked, fleshy roll around the old man's ankle. They don't match the board shorts and faded Ron Jon T-shirt he's wearing. He reminds the boy of the men and women they see along King Street with their knapsacks and cardboard signs, the ones his mother hurries him past.

The old man's smile is brilliant, eyes bright as the South Carolina sun.

"Dad?" the boy's mother asks.

The old man pulls her into a hug, chin resting on her shoulder. His mother's hands flutter over the old man's back before landing and she wrinkles her nose. The boy has seen this look on her face before, mostly in the kitchen when she peels back a corn husk to find a worm inside, but also when she's bent over her books, notes scattered around her as she looks for something she needs.

The hug runs long, and his mother's hands keep lifting from his back as she stands, bent into the hug, the old man's arms crumpling her into a new and uncomfortable shape. As soon as she puts her hands on his shoulders and starts pushing away, the boy's father slips an arm around her waist, pulling her back as he sticks his other hand out.

"It's nice to meet you."

His father's words drawl smooth and elegant in a way his mother calls genteel. She tries to emulate it some-times, making the boy laugh and his father groan and try to hide his smile.

"Stop," he'll say. "That's awful." And then she laughs too.

But the old man ignores the offered hand, staring at the boy instead. There's a looseness to his eyes that both-ers the boy, the way they push up against his eyelids.

"Married a Southern boy, I see," his grandfather says.

The summer night feels heavy, and the boy fidgets un-der his long gaze, searching for a bit of air to dry the dampness from his skin. "Where are you from?"

The old man laughs, a full belly laugh with his mouth wide open. The boy stares. He's never seen anyone with a tongue and throat so white.

"Oh I like you," the old man says.

His father drops his hand to his side. "Mr. Franklin—"

His grandfather's gaze snaps to the boy's father. "That's not my name." He nods his head at the boy's mother. "Not her name either."

Teach grumbles at the boy's side.

There's a long moment, the boy's fingers caught in Teach's fur, and then the old man finally sticks his hand out. "Sorry about that. Getting old and my eyesight's not so good in the dark."

His father hesitates before taking the old man's hand, the muscle in his jaw twitching.

"Sure. Yeah, sure. Nice to meet you, Mr. . . ."

The old man's smile makes the boy uneasy, though he doesn't know why.

The conversation comes like the stirring of thick marsh water when something ancient and slow moves at its bottom. The boy slips away, skimming his hand along the side of the station wagon until he gets to the back. The car is dirty, like someone raced it up and down the back roads between the cotton and peanut fields. The boy drags his finger through the dust on the window, first drawing his name and then sketching a picture of Teach. The light shines through the window into the back and the boy catches sight of a surfboard fin, the board stretching across the top of the back seat.

Pressing his nose to the glass, hands cupped around his eyes, he peers inside, looking for a suitcase or maybe a duffel like his father carries on field trips, but there's no luggage. Just the surfboard and a short wet suit. There's a large irregular lump beneath the neoprene, the board's Velcro ankle strap stuck to a patch of carpet. He continues around the car, brushing the edge of darkness as he tries to get a better angle, but from there he can only see a baby's car seat. The front of the car is littered with fast-food bags, the passenger seat full of those little salt packs they give you at the drive-through.

He takes Teach's collar, pulling gently as he starts back toward his parents, but draws up short as the old man steps in front of him.

"Hey there. Give your grandfather a hug."

The boy has the same nose wrinkle as his mother, though it has less to do with worms and more to do with hugging.

When the old man's too-soft arm brushes along his cheek, he smells low tide and fresh bait. He takes the boy's chin, turning his face one way and then another before using his thumb to lift the boy's eyelid, making his eye water, and the boy steps back, turning his head away.

His mother grabs his shoulders, pulling him back against her. He tries to squirm away, but she grips tight, pinching.

"Where've you been, Dad?"

His grandfather pats his tummy, scratching through the T-shirt. "Been serving as ship's cook, but that's a story for later. Invite me in for a cup of coffee."

And just like that, his grandfather pushes his way into their lives.

———

The next day, Teach and the boy sit under the mossy trees sharing a thermos of Tang and a cheese and brown sugar sandwich, the world hot, insects buzzing around them. The old man spots them while coming up from the beach, bent as if he carries the heat on his back. Teach sits up from his lazy sprawl and rumbles a deep and rusty growl.

Standing before them, backlit by the sun, the old man looks dark and endlessly hollow. He sits by the boy, sagging into the shade, shirtless, his face tan and smoother than the boy's—every bit of personality scoured away. He's still wearing his dress shoes and they look even weirder now that he's shirtless. The boy's hands twitch, fingers digging into his sandwich with the urge to reach out and pinch the roll of flesh above the top of the old man's shoes.

The boy parses the way his grandfather smacks a mosquito away, the way he leans back on his hands and stretches his legs out, the tips of his shoes in the sun still. He catalogs the old man's blunt, worn fingers and the tilt of his mouth looking for his mother's long silences and her wide, pretty smile, or his own constellation of freckles and the gap between his front teeth.

"Eating lunch?" his grandfather asks.

"Yes, sir."

The old man pulls a seashell from his pocket, rolling it between his fingers, pausing to trace the whorls and ridges with his thumb. His grandfather seems to catalog him, too, gaze roving from the riot of hair on the boy's head down to his hands then back up over his skinny chest and knobby collarbones. The boy waits—polite, like he was taught—but his grandfather doesn't say anything else, so he asks the most important question first.

"What's it like being a ship's cook?"

The question seems to delight the old man. He puts his hand on the boy's shoulder, jostling him, and Teach goes stiff at the boy's side.

"Mostly it's no good. You're always down in the belly of the ship, where you can't even smell the ocean or taste the salt on the air."

The hand feels hot on his shoulder, even through his shirt.

"What's your mother feeding you?"

"Sandwich." The boy shows him the filling.

His grandfather's whole face crinkles into harsh lines.

"No wonder you're scrawny."

"It's my favorite."

The boy starts to look down at his sandwich, but his grandfather ducks his head, holding eye contact so he can't look away.

"Your favorite, huh? What else do you like to eat?"

"Pizza and macaroni and spinach balls."

"Spinach balls?" The old man frowns. "You don't like hamburgers and hot dogs?"

The boy shrugs. "Yeah, they're okay."

His grandfather leans in close and the boy scrunches his face in anticipation of a kiss to his head but it never comes, though he feels the brush of something against his hair. The boy stills and Teach shifts, the fur on the dog's lower legs stiff—almost sharp—against his knee. The old man backs off and pats his other shoulder.

"Well . . . you're young yet. You'll grow into your taste buds."

The boy runs a hand through his hair, checking if the old man put something in it, but it's just his hair, stiff with dried saltwater. He shrugs, hoping to dislodge his grandfather's hand, and when that doesn't work, he drops his shoulder. But the hand lays against him limp as seaweed.

The old man's eyes gleam bright as midday sun on water. "Something wrong?"

"No, sir."

His grandfather stares at him, unblinking, the shell in the old man's hand constantly moving, his smile wide and white. The boy shifts in the grass, nudging Teach over and looks toward the house, but the afternoon is still, the door and the windows closed against the heat.

"You like to swim, I bet," his grandfather says.

"Yes, sir."

"Like to dive down deep?"

"Sometimes."

"We'll have to go swimming together."

The boy picks at the crust on his sandwich, rolling it into little pills, brown sugar dropping onto his shorts. It reminds him of the way his grandfather rolls the shell between his fingers.

The old man's station wagon sits alone in the drive, the sun reflecting off the chrome bumper.

"Will you teach me to surf?" the boy asks.

The old man blinks at him. "Surf? Don't know how to surf. Maybe you can teach me."

"But I just asked you to teach me."

"Well, that's a conundrum, isn't it? I guess we'll just have to teach each other."

The boy looks back at the station wagon. "Why do you

have a surfboard if you don't surf?"

The grandfather shrugs. "It's not mine. You have a girl-friend?"

"Ew. No."

He picks the crust off his sandwich, feeding it to Teach. "Who does it belong to?"

"Nobody you know."

"Oh." The boy looks down, watching an ant crawl through the grass.

"That Jolly Roger hanging over your bed, that's like your mom, you know, always interested in pirates."

He wipes dog drool on his swim trunks. "Yeah. She tells the best stories."

A serpentine warmth trails down his spine, making him shiver, but when he reaches back there's nothing there.

"Yeah? What kind of stories?"

He shrugs again. "Like Madame Cheng."

"Madame Cheng?"

"She led the Red Flag Fleet after her husband died."

His grandfather snorts. "Sure."

His father says if he can't understand a problem, it might be a proximity issue, that he might need to get some distance from it, and if that doesn't work, get closer to it. His grandfather sits right there—almost on top of him—and is still confusing.

"Pirates were real big on loyalty. You know what happened when someone wasn't loyal?"

"No, sir."

"Well, if they didn't outright kill you, they'd maroon you. And Old Bart, sometimes he'd slit your nose and ears first."

The boy imagines marooning Leonard, a boy in his class, maybe during recess—tattlers definitely lack loyalty—but he's not sure where they'd put him, and he'd just tell on them anyway.

The old man moves his feet, the hard soles on his shoes *tap, tap, tap*ping as he brings the toes together.

"Are you homeless?" the boy asks.

The shell stills in his grandfather's hand, his gaze jerking from Teach to the boy. "Is that what your mother told you?"

The boy leans away. "No."

His grandfather narrows his eyes and gestures toward the house with his chin, the nod sharp and tight. "She's a regular jawfish, ain't she? Miss Polly Perfect. Hanging her laundry on the line out back. Sweeping the porch. I bet she bakes, doesn't she. She bake apple pies? Peach?"

The boy leans into Teach, the sandwich gripped in his fist, palm sticky, gnats flitting around the warm brown sugar. Teach stretches forward, nose quivering in the air.

Usually, it's his father who does the baking. He doesn't

know why, but he doesn't say that.

The shell disappears into his grandfather's fist, his knuckles going white as he squeezes. The sun changes angle, the light hitting his grandfather so he almost glows.

The boy shifts to get up, sandwich crumpled on the ground already swarming with ants. The old man clamps his hand back down on his shoulder, keeping him still.

"Now don't go running off. You've got a whole childhood on me."

Teach bares his teeth, upper lip quivering as he inches forward until his front paws rest on the ground between the boy's legs, and the old man glares at the dog.

"That dog has a temper."

Thunder rumbles in the distance and dragonflies flit over the grass.

The boy wraps an arm around Teach's neck. "No, sir. Not normally."

He's never noticed before how white the screen door looks or how dark the porch behind the screen seems.

"It's going to storm. I should probably go back inside."

His grandfather shakes his head. "We got time yet. That storm is still way out over the Atlantic. You know, you look like your mother."

The boy frowns down at his lap. Other than the color of his eyes, it's not true. Not one person has ever said he looks like his mother.

"She says I look like Dad."

The old man waves his words away. "All women say that. It makes the man feel secure."

"Why?"

"Because. If you look like your dad, then he knows you're his kid."

"Oh." He tries to work his way through that and finds he can't.

"You and I, we're family," the old man says.

The boy nods, one hand knotted into Teach's fur as he watches the front door of his house.

His grandfather slides his hand up the boy's shoulder to the back of his neck. "You know, being a boy in our family is special. The sea runs in your veins."

Teach tenses just before he lunges, and even though the boy catches him around the neck, he's sure the dog has put teeth into the old man, but his grandfather has rolled away—a good five feet between them now.

The world sits hot around them, his ears filled with the whoosh of blood like the rush of sea over sand.

The air ripples around the man like heat off asphalt, and even with the distance between them, the boy can feel it stinging the right side of his body, tendrils of it making their way up through his hairline. He shivers and tries to brush the feeling away, Teach snarling and shaking.

Their blue Thunderbird rolls up the drive, setting the

world in motion again. His father parks in front of the house, opening the suicide doors and taking out the groceries. The door to the house also opens, his mother stopping on the porch steps, hand up to shield her eyes from the sun. When she spots the boy she hurries down the steps, calling him over.

"Hey," his grandfather says, tossing the shell into the dirt by the boy's feet. The boy picks up the shell, cradling it in his hand. "Everything else is just water, boy."

Thermos forgotten, he tugs Teach with him back across the lawn, through anthills and fallen pine needles, away from the old man.

———————

That evening, his grandfather watches him from the rocker on the porch as he and Teach lie on the lawn—Teach humming along with the cicadas' song—watching as they chase lightning bugs in the fading light, watching as his father shows him roly-polies—*Armadillidium vulgare,* his father says—watching as he captures large, fuzzy moths so he can set them free and make wishes for tomorrow, watching until he's made to go inside and get ready for bed.

His mother, too, sits by the door, still and silent, following the boy's every move. The boy doesn't notice.

He's too busy thinking about how roly-polies curl into a protective ball at the slightest touch, and the carnival coming to town next month. He doesn't know yet he won't get to go.

He doesn't mean to see his mother take herself apart, but he can't find Teach's treats and his parents' bedroom door stands open. He watches her reflection in the bathroom mirror as she removes the wire from her mouth, taking three upper teeth with it. When she sees him, they stare at each other through the mirror, his face hot. There's a clatter as she drops the teeth into the sink and turns, hand in front of her mouth.

He's woozy, caught up in the sharp orange scent of her perfume and the slight, woodsy smell of Skin So Soft. Her silk robe hangs open, the white slip beneath matching her pale face. With her black hair piled loosely on top of her head, the escaped strands wet where she's washed, she looks young, her eyes large and startled in the bright bathroom light.

"I thought you were in the tub," she says.

He shakes his head. Catching his shoulder, she turns him around, the arm of her robe brushing his cheek, cool silk against his flaming skin.

"Go. I'll come in a minute."

He looks back as she pushes him out and closes the door in his face.

His life has been full of stories. His mother drawing forth history from the ocean. His father excavating the past from the land. But tonight there are no tales. His mother sits by his bed, quiet, staring out the window into the dark. The teeth are back in her mouth, but she still looks different.

Closing his eyes, he turns onto his side, his back to the room, and buries his face in Teach's fur. And Teach, well, he holds on tight in that way only a dog can.

II

Sitting on the floor, the boy draws islands on the paper in his lap, large islands and small islands. He draws until they touch and become peninsulas, land rising up from the water. In the bottom left-hand corner, he draws a compass. In the upper right, a Jolly Roger. He pauses, staring at the lines, pencil hovering over the paper.

He huffs and unfolds his legs, stretching them out beneath the coffee table. Behind him, their fuzzy calico couch sticks to his back, and he leans forward to let the sweat dry.

Beside him, Teach's tail whacks his leg, his nose stuck under the couch snuffling dust bunnies. The boy lets his head fall back onto the seat, looking up at where his father sits on the couch next to him, and studies his dark hair and the sharp line of his nose, the way his brow wrinkles as he reads from the book on his lap. His pen scratches across the legal pad on the couch beside him. It's funny how he can write straight lines without ever looking at the paper, his pen moving smoothly from line to line. It's hard, the boy has tried, but his words end up dangling and running into each other.

"Dad?"

"Mm-hm."

His father doesn't look up from his papers.

"Do I look like Mom?"

"Mm-hm."

The boy waits. The sun streaming through the large double windows on the front of the house has the room too warm, the ceiling fan above them stirring the air like soup. Teach rolls to his side, panting hard. In the kitchen, he can hear his mother opening and closing cabinet doors.

His father stops writing and blinks down at him, eyes large behind his glasses. "Some, yes. There's a bit of her in your chin, I think."

The boy rubs at his chin.

He studies the boy's face. "Does that bother you?"

"No, sir."

His father does that thing where he doesn't say anything. He just keeps looking at the boy, the moment stretching between them like saltwater taffy in the sunshine. The boy looks away.

Teach turns, putting his head in the boy's lap, on top of his drawing pad.

His father moves the book—a large, heavy thing with

words highlighted in yellow and notes in the margins—placing it on the coffee table and resting his elbows on his knees.

"But?"

The boy sits forward to look at the book, eyes skimming the page as the silence grows between them again. His mother says his father is a born fisherman, content to outwait the deepest sea dwellers.

He shrugs. "Grandfather said I look like her."

"Well, we tend to see what we're looking for. You look like both of us."

The boy goes quiet, struggling to articulate something he doesn't understand.

His father rests his hand on his shoulder. "Why did that bother you?"

He shakes his head, pausing on a word in the book, finger tracing over it. "What's a lepidoptera?"

His father pulls off his reading glasses and puts them on the table. He hesitates, still watching the boy, before turning back to the book. "Do you remember the scientific classification system we talked about?"

"Yes, sir. King Phillip Came Over For Great Soap."

"Mm-hm. And that stands for?"

The boy stares at the entrance to the kitchen, trying to recall. "Kingdom . . ."

There's salt on the floor, tiny white grains that stick to

his legs and his fingertips when he presses them to the parquetry, and the rich smell of spaghetti sauce and garlic lingers in the air. The boy's stomach grumbles.

The back door opens and closes, the deep baritone of his grandfather's voice rumbling, his mother answering, voice high and light.

Teach sits up and sneezes before getting up and walking around the coffee table to lie on the boy's other side, where the floor is cooler.

"Phylum, class, order, family, genus, species. Lepidoptera is the order that the Polyphemus moth belongs to." His father taps the picture.

"Sorry," the boy says.

His father regards him, head cocked to the side. "For what? Not remembering? Don't apologize for that. Remember what I said about understanding?"

"It takes time and study."

"It does. Just don't give up and you'll be fine." His father hesitates again and then rests his hand on the boy's shoulder. "You can always talk to me. You know that, right?" He looks toward the kitchen. "No matter what."

The boy nods, frowning.

The phone rings once, twice, and his father stands, raising his voice. "I'll get it." He rests his hand on the boy's head.

The boy looks down at his unfinished map.

His grandfather's voice rises in the kitchen, the deep rumble edged sharp and hard. Before the boy can get up, the old man steps into the living room and stops, scowling at him.

"Why are you rolling around on the floor with that thing? You're not an animal. Get up, go wash your hands."

The boy gets up off of the floor, Teach glued to his side. He glances in the kitchen as he walks by, seeing his mother standing by the stove, a dish towel wadded between her hands.

———————————

The cave sits where marram grass meets sand, the ocean rushing toward its entrance. During low tide the path glimmers with bits of shell and shifting sand. Here the grass grows wild and the trees in the forest on his right are a twisting respite from the sun.

The boy has explored caves with his father, but not this cave. This cave, his father says, is dangerous. There are caverns that drop sudden and deep into the earth, flooded chambers that never dry out. It reminds him of a seashell—the way he can hear the ocean echo at its entrance. Its darkness is absolute. The cave real and raw, unlike the caves at La Jolla with their lights and pathways and tourists. It probably stills holds its secrets. Maybe even part of a ship that washed in during a storm. There could be treasure, gold doubloons and jewels in a real chest of iron and wood instead of the cigar boxes his father gives him.

He looks down at the box in his hand, his treasure rattling against the cardboard as he tips it to the side, tucking it deep down into the hole where the sand stays cold and damp. He buries it as close to the cave as he can without going inside, weighing whether it's deep enough to stay safe from the tide.

The sea always rushes in, greedy for the land. His father says that one day—a bazillion years ago—a fish grew legs and walked on the land for the first time. And as funny as he thinks a fish with legs would look, he wonders how the sea felt when her inhabitants started walking away. He wonders if maybe that's why she keeps eating away at the land, trying to take back what it stole.

Teach returns from exploring the marram grass, nosing the sand as he inspects the burial spot. But it's the clatter of rock inside the cave that catches the boy's attention, the wheezing in and the breathing out of the wind, the entrance a dark maw. He catches a whiff of something rotten, like seaweed washed ashore and left to bake in the sun.

Gooseflesh breaks across his arms, a shiver along his spine that doesn't belong in the South Carolina heat. He holds his breath, waiting. If he stares at the dark long enough, he sees something move. A trick of his brain, his mother says when he calls her in to check his closet.

Teach thrusts his head under the boy's hand, nosing against him, herding the boy home, watching over him as he always does.

———————

Early one Friday morning they load up the car with his father's tools: a shovel, a trowel, a couple of buckets, and a sluice pan. There's a cooler packed with bottles of water, cans of A&W Root Beer, sandwiches, and pretzels with peanut butter. The boy sits in the back with his grandfather while his mother and father sit in front, his mother's hair tied back into a ponytail, her shoulders and arms still pale from the winter. They make a quick stop at the Mace Brown Museum of Natural History, where his father left his collection permit. And then they head up, out of the lowlands, to Horry County, to the Waccamaw River.

There are rules when it comes to field trips. Rule one: the boy must always listen to his mother and father. Rule two: his father always does the laundry after a field trip. And rule three: his mother always chooses the music. It's a three-hour drive up the 701 to the

Waccamaw National Wildlife Refuge—their trip fu-
eled by James Brown, Paul Simon, and Cat Stevens—
the trailer and skiff rattling where it trails behind them
like a gator's tail.

His father is all easy grins, elbow hanging out the window. The boy reckons his father likes teaching all right,
but it's the field trips he really loves, getting out in the silt
and mud, combing through the shale and sand. The boy
buries treasure. His father digs it up.

His grandfather sits still beside him, an old straw hat
on his bald head. He doesn't say much, and when the boy
tries talking to him, he answers in monosyllabic replies
and curt grunts. So the boy gives up, wondering why the
old man came in the first place if he didn't want to be
there. If he hadn't come, Teach could have.

They bypass the white, sandy trails peppered with
copper-colored pine needles, the tourist areas full of hik-
ers and bird watchers, driving deep into the refuge, down
into the land of foxes, lynx, and bears.

The boat ramp is little more than a worn-down,
muddy spit. His father turns the car carefully, backing the
trailer to the water's edge, lining it up so all his mother
has to do is slowly back it into the water.

His mother eyes the area when she gets out of the car,
lips pinched. The waterway is narrow and swampy, hardwood trees crowding the bank and growing up out of the

water—ancient sentinels that say do not pass. The water is still and dark. The buzz of mosquitoes almost loud enough to hear. She grimaces and shakes her head. "I think we're just going to stay in the car."

His father finishes up with the trailer and dusts his hands against his pants. "You sure? It'll be a couple hours at least, maybe more. That's a long time to sit in a hot car."

She nods. "I'll keep the air horn close by."

The boy hangs out the window. "Mom!"

She climbs into the driver's seat. "Son!"

The boy grunts and flops back into the seat, arms crossed over his chest. He hates it when this happens. When they get where they're going and his mother decides that she doesn't like the looks of something, so they have to stay behind while his father goes on an adventure.

She starts backing the car up, his father standing out of the way, directing her.

His grandfather twists, looking out the back window. "You should let me do that."

"I've got it, Dad."

"You're turning too far left."

She puts on the brakes and just sits there until his father calls from outside, "Everything okay?"

The boy climbs forward so he's halfway hanging over

the front seat, trying to get a look at his mother.

"Sit back." She starts backing toward the water again, inching the boat in.

His grandfather sighs. "Since when are you afraid to get into a boat?"

"I'm not afraid of getting in a boat," she says.

The boy scoots forward, fingers digging into the back of the front seat. "I could help Dad, though."

She arches a brow. "You could get bitten by a cottonmouth."

"If you'd let Teach come, he could've bitten the cottonmouth."

"There once was an—"

"Ew, Mom, no."

"What? You like that story."

The moment the car comes to a standstill his grandfather opens the door and gets out. "We'll all go."

There are rules for field trips, and the most important is that when it comes to what the boy can and can't do, his mother has the final say. For a moment, the boy and his mother sit looking at each other, and then the boy jumps out of the car and runs to the boat.

His father hands him a bucket, his tools tucked inside. "Thought you were staying here?"

"No, sir. Grandfather said we'll all go."

His father frowns and turns back to the car, but his

mother is still in the driver's seat, his grandfather bent, looking in the window.

"Hold on to those," his father says. "Don't go near the bank."

The boy watches his father head back toward the car and then turns to look at the water. The swamp looks like something from one of his books, a place where someone might go to hide or maybe sink a chest of gold.

When the adults come back, they're all quiet, his mother stiff. His grandfather walks right up to the bank and squats, stirring the water with his hand. He gets a handful and brings it to his nose, sniffing before making a face and letting it go.

"Freshwater. What are you hoping to find in here?"

"Bivalves, mostly." His father holds his mother's hand as she steps into the boat and then lifts the boy in. His grandfather gets in, and his father follows, pushing away from the bank with the wooden oars. "Specifically, the Waccamaw spike."

His mother sits in the middle of the boat, holding on to the boy like he might fly away.

His father turns to the boy. "The Waccamaw spike is found only in this river. It has two kinds of teeth. Hinge teeth and pseudocardinal teeth. The pseudocardinal teeth protect the animal by making it harder to open the shell."

"Shell? You saying we came all this way for clams? If that's what you wanted for dinner, I could've caught us some without the drive," his grandfather says.

The corners of his father's lips quirk up before he shakes his head. "Not clams, and we're not eating them. They're threatened."

The boy's mother brushes a stray wisp of hair from her face. "He studies them."

"Threatened by what?" his grandfather says.

His father grins real quick and then looks away, clearing his throat. "Threatened by extinction."

The boy's mother gives his father a tiny head shake.

His grandfather narrows his eyes and rubs his jaw. "Studies them."

He mumbles something else, but the boy doesn't understand it. He thinks maybe his father doesn't either. The humor is gone from his father's face, leaving behind an irritated look he's only seen from him a few times before, usually when he's talking about work stuff—politics, he calls it.

His father takes a deep breath and gives the boy a tight smile. "No motor here. We have to row our way in. You ready?"

"Yes, sir."

It's slow progress, but the deeper they get into the trees, the more magical the place seems. The water is so dark they can't see beneath it, just the scum and algae his father stirs around as they row their way in. It smells awful, like rotten eggs and decay. It seems inhospitable, but like death in the summertime, life is everywhere. The animals are the boy's favorite thing. They see herons and egrets, turtles sunning themselves on logs, and deer bounding along the drier land.

His father keeps up a running commentary, the boy full of questions. His father smiles and answers what he can, telling him they'll look up the rest when they get home.

Whether it's his father's kind smiles or his warm, easy drawl, his mother eventually relaxes a little. But his grandfather doesn't. He sits stiff at the front of the boat, his gaze fixing to every movement, every swish of water and every beat of a bird's wing.

They make stops along the way, his father hopping out to examine this log or that log, inspecting anything a mollusk might attach itself to. They may be there specifically for bivalves, but his father is curious—and reckless, his mother says. She hates this part, tensing up every time he gets out of the boat. The boy watches everything he does. The way he combs through the silt and debris, going from shallows back to the bank. At one point his father stops, standing straight, and then climbs higher up the bank, white bucket in hand. "Throw me that rope."

The boy scrambles to do as he's asked, and the father

anchors the boat to a tree so they won't float off. "Hang tight. I need to check this out."

The boy starts to climb out of the boat. "I want to go."

His mother grabs his arm and pulls him back down. "Absolutely not."

The boy watches his father until he disappears and then turns back to his mother. "Why won't you ever let me go with him?"

She gives him this pinch-lipped look and then turns away. "Because it's dangerous."

"You always say that."

"It's always dangerous."

The boy huffs. "When will it not be dangerous?"

"When you're old enough."

"I'm old enough."

She digs around in the cooler until she finds a bottle of water and cracks it open, drinking from it.

"When will I be old enough?"

She turns, looking toward the land where his father disappeared. "What's the rule of field trips?"

"It's not fair."

She keeps her back to him. "Life isn't fair."

His grandfather chuckles and puts his arm across the boy's shoulders. "No use arguing, son. That's just a mother's way. They'll hold on long as they can. Besides, the most interesting stuff is here." He turns the boy so he's looking deeper into the swamp. "Look over there. What's that?"

At first, the boy doesn't see anything, just black water and logs, but then the water moves, a yellow eye blinks. "Gator!"

The old man chuckles. "Yeah, gator. See how most of him stays under the water, just his eyes and snout sticking up. That's an excellent bit of camouflage. The ability to hide in plain sight is incredibly useful. In the ocean, many animals camouflage themselves." He twists, digging into the cooler for water. "That's kind of a small gator. Think you could take him?"

The boy grins. "Sure."

"Go get him."

His mother grabs the back of his shirt like the boy might actually jump in.

"Dad."

His grandfather finishes off the bottle of water and sticks it back into the cooler, grabbing another. "What?"

"Don't put ideas in his head. He doesn't need you goading him on."

His grandfather eyes her up and down. "Just teasing the boy."

She glares at him. "Like you teased Ian."

The boy looks between them. "Who's Ian?"

The muscle in the old man's jaw twitches and he points toward the land with his chin. "He's sort of odd, isn't he?"

His mother starts biting her thumbnail, turning to look for the boy's father. "He might think that of you."

His grandfather's lip curls and then he sniffs, looking away and smiling. "You didn't get as far as you think, you know."

She bends, grabbing the air horn from the bottom of the boat, holding it in her lap.

"I'm not sure what you mean."

His grandfather puts his hand on the boy's shoulder, smiling at him. "This one here, he's a chip off the old block. Aren't you?"

The boy looks at his mother and then back to his grandfather. "I guess so. Who's Ian?"

His grandfather winks at him and pulls him into his side.

His mother fumbles with the air horn, and for a moment, the boy thinks she's going to use it, so he tenses, ready to cover his ears.

His grandfather eyes the canister. "What is that thing?"

"Air horn. We use it to call Dad if he needs to come back real quick."

His grandfather huffs and looks around. "Not sure why you're clutching that thing. There's no danger. You're safe. You're dry. It's just the three of us here in a boat. Just family."

His mother runs her tongue over her teeth. The boy doesn't like the way she's looking at him, like she doesn't know who he is. There's a sudden thrash of water, a *thunk,* and the boy turns to see the gator *thwack* a tree with its tail again and again. A small tuft of feathery white fluff falls into the water, and then another. The gator turns, snapping his teeth around the egret chicks, and again, chewing before it tilts its head back and swallows. Above them the mother circles, her grating, throaty cries filling the swamp as she watches the gator eat her young.

His mother uses the air horn. The sudden blast of noise startles the boy, and he loses his balance, his grandfather catching him before he topples in.

"Fucking hell." His grandfather snatches the air horn away, tossing it into the bottom of the boat, mouth open wide like he's getting ready to yell. "What's wrong with you?"

It takes a minute for his father to get back. He comes running, looking frazzled. "What? What is it?" He looks around, but it's just the three of them now; the gator moved on.

"We need to go," his mother says.

His father wades into the water. "Why?" He looks around again. "I just need a little more time. You won't believe what I found. There's a space a couple hundred yards back where the underbrush clears out. Honey,

S. L. Coney

there's still some cabin foundations, and look." He sets his bucket in the boat and the boy moves closer, trying to see what he's found. His father brings out a stone, dirt still clinging to it. It's irregular, the surface wavy and smooth. The boy has seen enough to know this rock was shaped by human hands.

"See this notch," his father says. "This is where a handle attached, this part, this was the cutting edge. And there's more, look here." He pulls out something that resembles his own pipe, but thinner, and clay colored. "This is . . . I don't think anyone has been here. They were probably slaves, hiding out here. This could be a huge find."

His mother won't look at the boy.

"I'm sorry. I have to go. We have to go. Now."

His grandfather scowls. "There's no need—"

"Now."

His father looks back toward the encampment and then turns, looking at the boy and the grandfather. The boy shrugs.

His father is unhappy about it, but he loads his finds into the boat, unties it, and gets everyone back to the car. They make a quick stop so his father can use a phone, and then they get back on the 701.

Their trip home is quiet, the radio off.

———

The house changes. His grandfather's pillow and blanket are always folded on the couch, so there isn't room for everyone to sit together. The small kitchen table where he and his father once dissected a frog stays piled with the old man's detritus: shaving kit, toothbrush, and keys. His father's record player gathers dust.

The boy finds those fast-food salt packets everywhere: stuffed between the couch cushions, the bathroom wastebasket, even between the pages of one of his father's books. He figures they should tell his grandfather they have saltshakers—a plain brown one with a wide base and a narrow top, and one shaped like a dolphin jumping out of the water that his mother calls kitschy and hides in the cabinet above the stove.

But the house isn't the only thing that changes.

Shadows move in with the grandfather. They trail behind his father like a fetch and nest beneath his mother's eyes. She grows thinner, paler. She stops smiling altogether. His father remains silent, distracted, as his wife slips away.

———————

The day the storm comes is almost a relief. For the past week the boy watched his father move through the house checking the Bermuda shutters, checking things the boy didn't even know about, like hurricane straps. He's watched his mother stare out the window as if she's reading their fate in the glass. And Teach, he has paced for days, stopping occasionally to stare out the screen door and whine, his body tense even at night when the boy curls around him.

The dark clouds loom in the distance and wind blows through the trees, whipping the Spanish moss like the long skirts Mrs. Jones wears when she comes to the library to tell stories of the Gullah Geechee people. The boy can feel this coming thing, a new weight, and though his tummy feels tight, there's a burbling rush that catches in his throat and makes him dig his fingernails into the wooden windowsills of the screened porch. It's the same feeling he used to get at the playground when he swung so high his feet touched the tree limbs and he hung, weightless, before plummeting back down.

Even with his eyes closed, he can see the sharp rise and deep trough of the waves, can feel the sea foam on the breeze and the tightness of salt on his skin.

His grandfather comes barreling out of the house, past the porch corner where Teach and the boy have tucked themselves to watch the world churn itself up. The old man pauses in the backyard, looking up just as the first drops of rain hit the screen—teasers, his mother calls them.

"Grandfather?"

The old man turns his face up, eyes closing as he breathes deep. "Can you feel the storm, boy? Feel all that power?" He turns, loping toward the ocean in his black dress shoes and board shorts, his bald head gleaming.

The boy watches him go, torn. Teach growls, his tail bristled, ears perked up.

Inside, the house remains dark, the shutters closed, the overhead light off. His mother carries a couple of coolers into the kitchen, both scratched and stained. The boy watches her put them on the counter by the sink and roll up her sleeves.

"Grandfather went down to the beach."

The moment he speaks, there's a twisty, smarmy feeling in his gut and he has to look away.

She pauses, water drumming against the hollow cooler.

"What?"

Leaving the cooler tipped on its side, she crosses by him, out the door, and onto the porch.

"Are you sure he went toward the beach?"

He steps out onto the porch behind her, Teach brushing by him to stick his nose against the screen door. Wind blasts through, whipping his hair back and bowing the screen in its frame. The boy catches her profile, the edge of her cheek, the wrinkle of her brow, and wishes he hadn't said anything.

She turns back into the house, the boy and Teach at her heels all the way up the stairs. She disappears into her bedroom, closing the door behind her. The boy stands at the top of the stairs, rubbing his hand against the newel post. Teach continues past him to snuffle at the bottom of his parents' bedroom door.

Back downstairs, the boy turns off the kitchen spigot and then crosses back to the door. The rain comes hard, slanting through the screen to wet the porch.

It feels like it rains forever before his father comes downstairs, into the kitchen, and sits at the table. He shoves his feet into his tennis shoes, their white leather discolored from miles and miles of beach and pavement.

His mother comes in, arms crossed, watching his father. The messy bun on her head makes her face look longer, thinner, and his father's maroon College of Charleston sweatshirt dwarfs her, the long sleeves pushed up to her elbows, neck showing her collarbone.

His father pushes past her, grabs his jacket from the closet, and then hurries back, dropping a hand to the top of the boy's head.

"Hold down the fort for me, buddy."

His mother catches up to him on the porch, taking his arm.

"Wait."

She can't seem to decide where to focus her attention—

out at the wind and rain, or on his father.

He takes her hand, holding it.

"I'll run down and back real quick."

The boy grabs his slicker from the closet.

"I'm going."

His father points at him, pinning him in place with his finger.

"No. Stay here and help your mother. I'll be back in a couple minutes."

"Please."

"No. You want to give your mother a heart attack? There's a lot left to do. Stay and help."

He leans in and gives her a kiss before pulling up his hood and stepping out.

The wind whips the door out of his hand, blowing it all the way back against the porch, wood against wood. He grabs it and pushes it closed.

"Latch it!"

His mother takes the door, squinting against the wind and rain, slipping the metal hook through the eye.

His father hurries across the yard, head ducked against rain that comes at him sideways. The white and gray world churns and roils, and soon his father disappears from view. Teach whines, pawing at the door, but the hook and eye hold fast.

The boy takes off his slicker and throws it on the couch,

watching as it slips onto the floor. He wants to kick it, to stomp on it. He balls his hands into fists, eyes stinging. He gives in and kicks the stupid coat and then makes himself stand still until he's sure he's not going to cry.

Turning back to the kitchen, he finds his mother poised—caught between rooms—staring at him. At least, he thinks she was. The moment after he turns, she turns as well, disappearing back into the kitchen.

He hesitates before following.

She has the water on again, scrubbing one of the coolers. With her hair up and her head bowed her spine protrudes—sharp—like she's all kinked up. Teach, exhausted from his nearly constant vigil, has stretched out by the cabinets, eyes closed, leg twitching as he dreams.

The little bit of light coming through the open door doesn't push the dark back so much as blend into it like some of the old black-and-white photos his father has—the ones of his father's father overseas in Germany and France, uniform on, gun on his back, a dog at his side. The rain hits the shutters like fingers tapping, asking to come inside, and the wind whistles around the corners, searching.

All a storm needs is a crack, his father says, to tear the whole thing down.

The boy flips the switch by the door, turning on the overhead light. His mother flinches, dropping the cooler, plastic banging against the cast-iron sink.

"Turn that off."

The snap of her voice stings, but he does as he's told and then stands there, waiting for her to tell him how to help.

"I have a headache," she says.

He watches Teach sleep, tempted to get down on the floor with him. His father would say he was sorry and then offer to get her something to take or tell her not to worry about what she's doing, to go lie down.

There's a gust of wind so strong it sounds like it's going to blow off the roof. Something bangs against the side of the house, making them both jump.

He crosses toward her, but she slips away to the other side of the room, digging into a cabinet, motions jerky—rushed. "Here," she says, standing on tiptoe. She pulls down a Tupperware bowl, a gouge furrowed along its thick, brick-red plastic, and sets it on the counter before moving to stoop at another cabinet. "Take that and put the eggs in it. Make sure to fasten it tight."

He starts collecting the eggs from the refrigerator, stealing quick glances at her. It's quiet in a way he's unfamiliar with. He misses the steadiness of her hands, so sure you believe she can fix anything. He misses her distracted joy as she writes and he misses the lilt of her voice as she sings along with the radio, the words leaving her tongue like birds in flight.

She's still scrubbing that same cooler even though it'll never be spotless; it's endured too many family outings to the beach, gone on too many camping trips, and sat through too many of his father's baseball games. He wants to take it from her, to make her stop scrubbing as if she could erase their history.

His hands feel cold, the eggs like lumps of ice.

"What does grandfather like to do?"

It takes her so long to answer that he starts to think maybe she's caught, wound too tightly, and this is all she can do now.

"He wasn't around a lot."

"How come?" he asks.

She pauses and he feels almost deaf in the sudden absence of the metallic scratch of the Brillo pad. His mother leaves the spigot running and crosses to the door with wet hands.

"He worked at sea."

"On a boat?" he asks.

"On an oil rig."

"What's an oil rig?"

She doesn't answer.

He forgets what he's doing, watching her watch their backyard.

"Why does he always wear those shoes?"

She grips the doorframe, suds trailing down the wood.

He thinks maybe she hasn't heard him, so he starts to ask again, louder this time.

"Grandfather wears—"

"I don't know."

The boy starts cataloging what he knows about his own father—and he feels like he knows a lot. He knows that as a child his father fell once, trying to swing from a vine, and knocked himself out; that his favorite breakfast consists of scrapple and cheese grits; and that his favorite coat is the blue parka with SAVE THE SNAIL DARTER in white across the back even though the front pocket ripped during a field trip and is now patched with a maroon square.

He doesn't understand how his mother can't know something so singular about her father.

There's another bang from outside, jolting the boy and his mother, and he drops an egg to the floor.

"Damnit." His mother's voice shakes.

"I'm sorry."

He bends and starts picking up the eggshell.

She holds the doorknob, forehead pressed to the frame. There's a fine tremble running from her shoulders down her arms. Closing the door, she turns, pausing when she sees the egg on the floor, the boy's hands full of broken shell.

"Stop. Just . . . go wash your hands."

The edges of the eggshell prick his fingers before they break.

She walks past him, back to the sink.

"Mom?"

"Go."

He hesitates, but she doesn't turn around, and she doesn't say anything else. It isn't until he's washing his hands that he notices he's bleeding.

Outside, the sky has gone from gray to a grape-soda purple, and neither his grandfather nor his father have come back. He looks to the kitchen once more and then grabs his slicker from the floor before slipping out the front door.

———————

He's drenched within the first few minutes outside, his slicker useless. He doesn't find his father or grandfather on his way down to the beach but it's hard to see. Several times he's startled, ready to run, when something huge and gray appears on his right, an alien creature to go with the alien sky. It isn't until he's brushed by some of the fur that he realizes he's off course, pushed toward the trees with their Spanish moss. With the wind whipping the branches, the trees are alive in a way they've never been before, their arms waving in the rage of the storm. They have a language, one spoken in a creaking tongue. The earth at their feet moves with their sway, making him stumble. There's a crack overhead like his father's bat against the ball. He feels the limb as it falls in front of him, leaves tickling his face as he falls backward. There's another crack and he skitters out, away from the trees and into the fury tearing them apart.

By the time he gets to the dunes, his muscles ache. He tries to shield his eyes, down on his knees as he searches for some sign of his grandfather, either the old man out in the waves or his shoes tucked into the scruff where he usually leaves them. When he does finally find them, the sharp toes protruding from the dune, he digs his fingers in, pulling at the shoes until they come free, but there are no other signs of his grandfather, or his father.

"Dad!"

He stands, eyes half-closed as sand pelts him like needles. The storm presses down on him and the waves reach for him, and the boy's heart beats hard and fast. He shouts, the noise full of his burning lungs, gritty eyes, and scoured skin.

"Grandpa!"

The wind howls louder, longer.

He looks to the cave, but water spills from the opening, foamy like the vomit of a drowning man.

The boy turns and runs back the way he came, but instead of heading toward the house, he turns right, approaching the rocky outcropping from the back. Up here, he can see much farther—the waves jumping and slicing, stretching forever, the world boiling beneath him. The rocks at the apex are slippery and the wind tries to shove him over, so he drops into a crouch, gripping the stone with his stinging hands. He can't go back, not without his father, not with his mother so tense, her edges no longer flush.

"Dad!"

He almost misses the shape rising from the waves, then nearly dismisses it as a waterspout, but it doesn't crest and fall, it doesn't swirl or move with the sea. It's the bald pate he recognizes first. His grandfather throws back his head and howls with the wind, arms up in the air as if summoning rapture.

The old man starts walking. The waves shove and push, they drive themselves against the rock, remaking the land, but somehow his grandfather keeps coming, walking toward shore.

Some of the tension drains out of the boy, leaving him weak and shaky.

He hears his name, distant and unreal, and he lets go of the rock, waving at the old man. "Grandfather!"

Then he hears Teach bark. The boy stands and turns. His father runs toward him, Teach in front, barreling at him, and the boy laughs. His father shouts at him, something about going to town.

"What?"

He has a second to see something beige and brown, something long, one end flapping, flying through the air at him like an uneven bird. Metal hits him with a solid crunch across his face. His fingers slip between chair straps, a moment of rubber against his fingertips, and pain explodes from his face back through his head as he's lifted up and back, airborne before plunging down.

He hits the water so hard it's like rock, and instead of sinking he's melting, body turned to jelly. He's too stunned to move, to hold his breath, and the saltwater burns his eyes, nose, and throat. Down, beneath the chaos, the sea rocks him toward sleep, urging him into peace. But instead of going darker, things lighten, the water turning from dense black to a foggy green. The boy sees his grandfather floating there, watching him, and then he catches movement to his right, a glimpse of four paddling legs and red fur, and then the light fades.

———

He wakes up in trouble. Only it's not normal trouble, it's delayed trouble, on account of him being in the hospital. He's seen his father look a lot of ways—dirty and bloody from falling off the side of a shale rock face, half-drowned when his boat capsized on the swollen Pee Dee River, sheepish and apologetic when the boy's mother yelled at him for trying to cross an old footbridge stretched high above the Clinch that bowed and creaked with his father's weight. But he's never seen him as ragged and worn as he looks sitting in the chair by his hospital bed.

Even his grandfather looks tired. The old man stands by the door, away from the windows, sagging against the wall like he might melt into the paint if given the chance. The old man watches him, a heavy scowl turning his eyebrows into one long fuzzy caterpillar.

The boy asks for his mother, his tongue stiff, his face throbbing like it'll crack open if he moves too much.

His father leans forward, squeezing his arm. "She's here, in the cafeteria," he says. "Your head hurt?"

It does. More than anything he can remember.

His father leaves, brushing by his grandfather like he's not there, and when he comes back it's not with his mother, but a woman in scrubs with teddy bears on them, and after a few minutes his head starts to feel more fuzzy than throbbing.

"Where's Teach?"

Words start coming easier, like the medicine oiled his tongue.

His father sits back in the chair, tapping his fingers against its padded arm.

"Dad, where's—"

"They don't let dogs in hospitals," he says.

The boy falls somewhere between asleep and awake, the fuzziness in his head leaching out to the world, until his dreams walk.

The thing that hit him, his father says, was a sun chair, one of the big, heavy ones they keep at hotel pools.

"I was looking for you," the boy says, and then sinks again, into real sleep, into the darkness where his face no longer hurts. But it's the first time he's slept by himself since Teach arrived, and he keeps waking up, searching for his warm body and soft fur, and he can't wait until he can go home.

———

The ride home is uncomfortable, his mother and father silent and distant in the front seat.

From the moment they leave the hospital, destruction litters their route. Water stands in the streets, people picking through broken glass and piles of soggy belongings as they try to recover what they can. Workers wade through in their Day-Glo vests, wrenching felled trees away from the road, sawing them down to manageable chunks.

The trip takes forever, his father driving slower and slower the closer they get to home. He wishes they would hurry—whatever his punishment will be, it can't be as awful as his parents' silence.

They turn into the drive, gravel crunching under the wheels before his father speaks.

"There's something we need to talk about."

Even with the awful heaviness of his father's voice, he starts to relax.

"We were really lucky that we were able to get you out of the ocean. Teach was brave when he jumped in for you, but the sea was rough and he—"

They come into view of the house to find Teach waiting for them by the porch, fur stringy and matted. His father hits the brakes, jerking the boy against his seat belt. He doesn't wait for whatever his father means to say next. Maybe he'll be in even more trouble for jumping out of the car, but at the moment he doesn't care. He runs the rest of the way up the drive and drops to his knees, hugging his best friend. His fur is stiff and dried into clumps and he's gotten into some sort of webbing, gauzy patches of silk caught in his fur. He smells musty but it doesn't matter. Teach has a right to be mad at him, too, but he leans against the boy, warm and solid as he licks his face, and the fear, it drains away.

———

Storms, the boy learns, may be brief, but their impact can change the land forever. Waves and wind erode the coastline, and trees, once strong and tall, fall—too damaged to continue. But his father is right. They are lucky. The tree that fell missed both their house and their car. They still have a roof over their heads and their windows are intact. The damage, his father says, is cosmetic, easy to fix.

At the top of the ladder, his father pauses his painting and leans slightly to the side, calling in through the open window, "Honey, you're going to have to take these curtains down. They keep blowing into my paint."

His mother answers from somewhere deeper in the house, and his father goes back to painting, sweeping the brush back and forth in long, even strokes. The ladder feels pretty steady, but the boy grips it harder, just in case.

The clouds sit low in the sky, a moody steel-gray cap, but it's humid, the air lying against their skin like a tongue. Around them, in the trees, there's a susurrus from the nesting birds, and Teach tenses, neck ruffling like a porcupine, but the boy doesn't look up. Already he has paint in his hair; he doesn't want it in his face too.

"I've got to lean out a little here. You have a good grip on the ladder?"

"Yes, sir."

The ladder shifts subtly under his hands, and he locks his elbows.

"What's a scrawny thing like you doing holding that ladder?" his grandfather asks.

The boy startles, jostling his father.

"Hey!" His father stops painting, gripping the top of the ladder.

His grandfather pushes the boy to the side, stepping into his place. He winks at him and then grins up. "No, now you just stay up there. Keep painting. Looks like you're doing a good job, though that last swipe is a bit uneven."

"Sorry," the boy calls up to his father.

His father stands stiff above them, looking down and dripping paint onto a pair of his old jeans. "I'd prefer you let him do this."

"Fall and break your neck, then where would you be? He's just a boy. Let him play."

"I don't mind," the boy says. "I can hold it."

"Nonsense. Go sit down," his grandfather says.

The boy forgets not to look up, blinking at his grandfather as he steps back.

His father looks wary, but eventually he nods at the boy and turns back to his painting. He's slow to start though, like he's looking for the place he stopped.

"Go on," his grandfather says.

The boy finds a spot in the grass just far enough away that he'll avoid falling paint. Teach settles beside him, ears perked as he watches too.

"Looks real professional," his grandfather says. "You could've made a living on this."

His father stops painting and twists his upper torso so he can look down. "What's that supposed to mean?"

"Just what I said. You're doing a good job."

His father stares down at the old man a bit longer before going back to work. "Yeah. Sure." There's a hitch in his brushstroke. "Someone has to do the hard thinking work."

"Nothing wrong with getting your hands dirty."

His father snorts, and the boy laughs. His grandfather glares at him and he quiets.

"What's so funny?"

The boy shrugs, plucking a piece of grass and wrapping it around his finger. "Nothing. Just . . . Dad is always dirty."

His father snorts again. "Not always."

His grandfather shifts his jaw to the side, studying him. "Dirty, huh?"

"Yeah," the boy says. "From hunting for fossils and specimens and camping. One time, a skiff he was on capsized, and it was so dark underwater that he couldn't tell which way was up, so he had to blow bubbles through his cupped hands and feel which way they rose."

His grandfather eyes him and then looks back at his

father. His father keeps painting, slower now, his stroke easier.

"How about you, do you camp?" His father dips the brush back into the can.

"No."

Turns out his grandfather, too, has the same nose wrinkle as the boy's mother.

His grandfather looks over his shoulder at him, mouth pinched. "I suppose you like to camp."

"Yes, sir."

They fall into silence, and even Teach starts to relax. The boy feels the weight of the heat, his eyelids heavy. He ends up lying in the grass, the world soft and hazy around him.

"Your paint will go on more even if you use the flat of the brush instead of the edge that way."

"I am using the flat of the brush."

"Nah, you're tipping it up."

The boy sits up, rubbing his eyes.

"I'm just trying to help," his grandfather says.

His father keeps on painting, lingering a bit on a section near the eave. "I appreciate that," he says eventually. He eyes the window again. "Honey, your curtains are going to be ombré."

"You know, she always had a thing for yellow," his grandfather says.

"Yeah?"

"She'd like that better, I think."

"She likes the green."

"You don't like yellow, is that it?"

"Yellow is fine. I just don't want it on my house. I like green. Everyone who lives here likes green. Don't worry about it so much."

There's an edge in his father's voice.

"My daughter likes yellow."

His father stops painting and just stands there, brush in hand. Teach walks over to the ladder and sits.

"It is remotely possible that she likes both yellow and green," his father says.

His father sounds distracted; his feet placed as far apart as the ladder will allow. After a moment, he starts painting again, but it's uneven.

His father says something the boy doesn't quite catch, and his grandfather shrugs, smiling up at his father.

"Just making conversation. You don't have to be rude about it."

"Yeah?" His father's brushstrokes hold a sharp edge.

His mother finally appears at the window, pulling the curtains into the house and then pausing when she sees her father. "Dad? I thought you were out on a walk."

"I came back."

The boy gets up and crosses over to the ladder, looking

up. The paint runs in places, the house seeping.

His father drops the brush and starts down the ladder. "I'm done for now."

His grandfather steps back, looking up at the house, and shakes his head. "It's going to be patchy if you don't finish now."

"Then I'll fix it later."

His father pulls the boy away. "Go on in the house and help your mother get the rest of the curtains down."

The boy goes but pauses on the porch, looking back at his father and grandfather, the way they've both squared their shoulders and the smile on the old man's face.

His father turns, spotting him on the porch.

"Go help your mom."

The boy leaves them. It isn't until later, when he's in bed, he and Teach whispering in the quiet, that he understands it's not so much about what his grandfather said as what he meant, and he understands that the surface of something can be entirely different from what's beneath.

———

History, his father says, has layers. There's the surface and then there's what lies beneath. There are, he says, varying points of view, the cultural meaning, and the sociopolitical events that happen during that time. You have to dig deep and you have to be careful that you don't destroy evidence as you go.

The boy stares out the kitchen window as he helps his mother do the dishes, wishing he was back at the site on the Waccamaw River with his father.

In the living room, the TV drones on, his grandfather stretched out on the couch. Teach pushes the kitchen door open with his nose, comes in from the porch, and stretches out on the floor, watching the boy as if he wishes he'd hurry up and get done so they can play in the fading light.

His mother is too quiet, focused on the dish in her hands, rubbing at it. She feels stiff beside him—thin and hard—as if everything soft and comforting has been stripped away, her layers disappearing.

He finishes drying a bowl and sets it on the cabinet. "Tell me a story."

She frowns, handing him another dish to dry. "The pirate Dixie Bull became known as the Dread Pirate because of an attack—"

"No. I mean a real story."

She stops washing, turning to him. "That is a real story."

"No, yeah, but I mean a story about you. Tell me about living in California."

His mother grabs another dish, rinsing it and then dunking it into the soapy water. She's quiet a long time before she begins, an emptiness that isn't quite filled by the drone of the TV or the chirp of insects outside.

"I'm not sure what you want to hear. It was a small town. Not much happened."

"Well, what did you do for fun?"

"I played. There were some kids in the neighborhood—"

"Ian?"

"No. Some girls, neighbors, classmates."

"Who was Ian?"

"No one you know."

"Well, yeah, that's why I'm asking."

She pauses, studying him before she looks away. "My brother."

The boy goes still, staring at her. He's never had an uncle before, an aunt either.

"Where is he? Does he live in California still? Can we go visit him?"

She shoots him a look that makes him go quiet. "I thought you wanted to know about what I did for fun."

"Well, didn't you ever have fun with him?"

"No."

That doesn't make any sense. If he had a brother, or even a sister, they'd have all kinds of fun.

His mother hands him another dish. "My friends and I, we'd swim or ride our bikes. I had a friend, Nikki. She used to stay over sometimes ..."

She goes quiet again, staring out the window and tonguing her upper teeth, making the false ones shift slightly before they settle back into place.

"But what about—"

"It's getting late. Go take your shower and get your pajamas on."

He looks out the window where the sun is setting, the fireflies just starting to twinkle in the night.

"It's not that late. I wanted to go—"

"Don't argue. Just go."

He stares at her a moment, but she won't look at him. Heading upstairs, he wonders, How careful do you have to be?

———————

The Tuesday before the Fourth of July, the boy goes upstairs looking for a book and hears his parents in their bedroom, the strident rise and fall of their voices pulling him to the door.

"What do you mean, he changed?" his father says.

"He changed. I don't know what else to tell you. His smell changed—"

The boy tugs at the thread on his shirt, unraveling the hem.

"Yes, that happens in puberty. You said he was twelve when it happened, right?"

The boy frowns. He won't be twelve until next week.

Teach, wanting to help, or maybe not liking what he sees when he looks at his best friend, scratches at the door. And those old doors with their loose iron doorknobs, they don't always latch so good.

His mother turns away when the door opens, wiping at her eyes and face, and his father's lips go tight and thin as he approaches.

"Did you find them?" His grandfather crests the top of the stairs. "Ah. Good. Dinner's on. Best get your asses downstairs." He pulls the boy into his side and winks at him. "Come on. You can help me get the drinks."

The boy glances back toward his parents' room as he's steered downstairs, Teach close on his heels.

In the kitchen, wrapped in the aroma of lemon and Old Bay seasoning, the boy turns his mother's and father's words over and over in his head, trying to make sense of them.

His grandfather catches his arm. "That's loyalty, boy. When your family's in trouble, you help out."

The boy knows his family is in trouble; he just doesn't know why.

Dinners are uneasy gatherings now, the family scattered amid the living room furniture. The boy's mother watches him, and his father watches her. The boy keeps his eyes on his plate. Mostly. He watches his grandfather out of the corner of his eye; straight on, he's a lie, just like Teach told him.

————————

His grandfather doesn't seem to notice that this family, once cohesive, has become jagged and raw. The old man, he sprawls where he sits, a book in his hand. He never reads, though; he just holds it open—smiling—never turning a page. And the boy realizes, finally, what's wrong with his grandfather's smile. When he's smiling, no one else is.

————————

There's a new ripeness to the boy, his feet uncoordinated, his hands dangling at his sides like overgrown fruit. He wakes in the middle of the night with his legs aching.

He's in the shower when he first notices how the air ripples around him like heat off asphalt. There's a fullness inside his chest—heavy and sore. He tastes copper on his tongue, and no matter how much he washes he smells like seaweed and brine.

The boy becomes aware of how hot the water is, and

how small the bathroom is. The steam thickens the air, making it hard to breathe. He backs out of the water, pressing into the yellow tile to cool his skin, and stays there until he's no longer dizzy.

Drying off, he watches his reflection from the corner of his eye, his mother's voice in his head.

He changed.

The boy squeezes his eyes shut and turns away.

———————

That night, after he turns off the light and climbs into bed, he lies there listening to the thunder roll across the sky in waves, crashing against the windows. The house holds a quietness that feels empty. He holds his breath, waiting for the murmur of a voice or the creak of a stair. He swallows the urge to call out to his parents, to ask for a drink of water or a closet check, a prickle along his scalp, goose bumps on his arms.

He concentrates on Teach's soft breathing, stomach gnarled into uneasy knots. Pressing his lips to Teach's ear, he whispers another secret.

"I'm scared."

Teach moves, lying on the boy's chest as if to weight him down. Knotting his hands into Teach's fur, he watches the window.

It's one of those bright summer days and the boy sits on the bluff overlooking the place he almost drowned. It's a good place to see the whole beach, but he never sees the old man. He's starting to suspect his grandfather is not on the beach at all but in the cave, in the dark, where the boy is not allowed.

The wind blows against his hot skin and the sun paints the water a briny green. The gulls caw to one another; the pelicans dip into the waves for their food. The boy wishes for a pelican beak, for feathers so he can soar over the waves and dip down and fill his mouth with water.

He's so dry.

Farther up the shore, a small plane banks and turns before it reaches them, trailing its black-and-red advertising banner behind it like an eel after prey.

He's about to stand to head home when he sees a gull stop mid-flight with a strangled caw, then plummet straight down, wings pushed upward with the force. The boy feels the bird hit the water, the same brutal smack he felt before he sank beneath the storm.

There's a hollow ringing in the boy's ears, the pounding of his heart in his fingertips like the crashing of waves on the sand. He replays it in his head, watching as the bird gets jerked down into the sea by some invisible force, like fishing but backward.

His stomach flips with the sensation of falling, and Teach puts his head in his lap. The boy holds on, Teach's tongue wet on his arm.

He still feels like he's falling when he stands and makes his way to the beach. The water feels so cool and soothing on his feet that he kneels there in the sand, letting the waves rush up over him, splashing into his face. He tastes the salt on his tongue, feels it burn his cracked lips as Teach paces behind him, a worried eye on the ocean.

The need is overwhelming, and he brings the water to his mouth, swallowing, swallowing, tasting every fish, every bird, every thing that's ever swum in the waters. Drinking, and then vomiting, and drinking again.

He stays until the sun almost touches the water, waiting to see if another bird gets jerked from the sky, but it doesn't happen again, and when he heads home—his skin hot and sore—the house is quiet, his grandfather still gone.

———

He finds his father out in the storage shed among the boxes of fossils and stacks of topographic maps. It's hot and dusty and one of his favorite places to be with his father. Surrounded by trilobites and ammonites, it's easy to imagine a different world, to feel the history beneath his feet. On hot summer nights, they sit just outside the shed doors and drink root beer floats. His father shows him relics—clay and bone. We live, we die, we feed the earth, his father says. We nourish it for new generations, leaving behind our legacy in the hopes it'll make the world richer for those who come after.

Now his father digs through a box of paper, the cardboard holding the lingering sweetness of his black cherry pipe tobacco. Teach sniffs and huffs, sticking his nose into corners like a ratter.

"Hey, kiddo."

The boy sits on a large upended bucket, its white plastic stained from countless field trips—dirt from forests, silt from rivers, mud from caves so quiet and cold you forget anything else exists.

"Something up?"

The boy shrugs, picking at a scab on his knee. He lets the silence build, teeth clenched until he can no longer swallow the words.

"Mom hates me."

His father stops and stares. Leaving the box, he leans his hip against the work surface, arms crossed. "She doesn't hate you. She could never hate you."

"She does."

It's in the way she won't make eye contact. The way she

no longer hugs him. The way she only speaks to him with her back turned.

"I've changed, too."

For several long moments, the only noise is Teach huffing and scratching at a box. The heat lies against their skin like damp corduroy, the air almost too thick to breathe. The boy finally looks away, scratching a mosquito bite.

"Come on. Let's go for a walk," his father says.

They head into the trees. The forest has always been his father's domain, the beach his mother's.

"How have you changed?" his father asks.

The boy shrugs, watching as Teach explores the roots of a magnolia, its blooms large as dinner plates, the air perfumed with its lemony scent.

"You've grown taller. You're breaking out. Are you washing your face?"

"That's not why Mom hates me."

"She doesn't—"

"What's wrong with me?"

"Nothing."

They stop, staring at each other.

"Look," his father says, "not everyone has a childhood like yours. Yours has been pretty good, yeah?"

The boy shrugs and then nods because it has. He knows it has.

"Your mom, hers wasn't so good, and she's remembering a lot right now."

"Why?"

This time it's his father who looks away, his hands on his hips as he stares at the stray beams of sunlight threading their way through the branches.

He puts a hand on the boy's shoulder and starts them walking again, deeper into the forest, through shafts of sunlight where gnats dance. Under thick branches where the world still feels quiet and ancient. Into the lowest of lowlands, where frogs sing and chirp and the brackish water of the marsh stirs before the sudden lunge and thrash for the gator's next meal.

"You remind her of someone."

"Grandfather."

"No."

"It's his fault."

His father catches his arm, stopping him. The boy huffs, pulling out of his grip.

"Did he say something to you?"

"No."

"Did Mom tell you that?"

"No."

"But it's his fault?"

He won't say any more; it seems wrong not to like his grandfather.

_____

The boy wakes to find his grandfather standing at the threshold to his room. Behind the old man, the moonlight throws strange shadows, long multifarious coils that wave and curl. The old man's head starts to glow, the dome fading, becoming jellylike. The boy stares, everything in him stilled and quiet, until his grandfather's eyes begin to sink into his head, forehead swelling up and down. Something inside the boy trembles and he has to look away, his blanket clutched in his fists.

The glow is small and golden at first. He tells himself to close his eyes, but he can't. He watches the light grow, watches it fall across his belongings, the model ship on his dresser throwing a giant rolling shadow, its sails billowing, and the Jolly Roger above his bed flaps and snaps in a breeze that smells of ocean and sweat. The room rocks and creaks, the boy's stomach rising and dropping with it. There are shadows he can't place, like his mother's tiger lilies unfolding—delicate and shy.

Something wet and meaty tears loose in his chest— roiling—slithering up his throat, flicking his uvula, grasping and pulling. He gags, eyes wide and watering, snot clogging his nose.

By his side, Teach doubles in size, fur standing on end, teeth longer, sharper in the moonlight. His neck rough stands up, sharp as porcupine quills. He jumps off the bed, his bark loud and savage, echoing around the room as he chases the grandfather away.

"Hey, what's going on in there?" His father pauses, looking into the room. "You okay?"

The boy nods, still staring at the wall. The light has faded, but the shadows remain, indelible.

His father continues down the hall after the grandfather.

Bending forward, the boy doubles over, swallowing and taking in great lungfuls of air. He presses his fingers against his eyelids until he sees white, just to make sure his eyes are still there.

III

Monsters, the boy thinks, should always be hungry and slavering, but his grandfather isn't. When his father cleaned up from the storm, his grandfather offered to help. And when his mother knocks a stack of laundry over, he pulls the washing machine out so she can get to the socks. He wears his human skin and he keeps his shadow-light hidden, but the boy knows what he is, and he thinks his father does too.

The boy's parents no longer retreat behind closed doors to argue, but it doesn't matter. Regardless of how the fights start, they all end the same way.

"He's my dad," she says, and the back door slams, the boy's father taking off down the long, twisting drive, his Pumas kicking up puffs of gravel dust as he jogs toward the road.

His mother continually twists her necklace—the one his father bought her for their eighth anniversary— around her index finger until the tip turns a bloodless white and the rest goes purple. His father keeps late nights reading in the hallway. He jokes with the boy about how night is the only time quiet enough, but the boy can see the circles under his eyes, and he can see the burden of his father's distance in the curve of his mother's shoulders.

His grandfather disappears down to the beach for hours, leaving them to wait for his return. His mother cleans—dusting, mopping, and vacuuming as if she can wash the pall away. His father starts keeping a couple fingers of Scotch close at hand.

The boy, he keeps waiting for it to happen again. He stares at the mirror, open-mouthed, his tongue and throat white and slick. In the bedroom, he presses at his eyelids and feels his face as Teach anchors him down. He runs his fingers through his hair, making sure it's still there, and then, in his nervousness, he starts plucking it from his head, creating tender little bald patches around his ears that burn when he goes swimming.

He thinks about telling his parents, or at least his father—he's pretty sure his mother already knows, that she can see the shadows in him—but in the end he doesn't. He is a secret, and he can't bear his father knowing the dirtiness of him.

While his father mows the lawn and his mother cleans the kitchen, the boy slips down the hall to his mother's study. The little office is stuffy and dim except for the muted sunrays that sneak through the closed plantation shutters, dust motes dancing in the beams. Teach stretches out as the boy pulls open drawers and combs the bookcases, but there are no false bottoms and no books on sea monsters.

He finds the notes about Madame Cheng on his mother's desk, written in her looping hand, some sections highlighted in dull yellow, others a neon orange. He no longer fits under her desk—his favorite spot to read—so he sinks to the floor by the chair, Teach's breath warm against his knee.

When he's done, he flips back to the beginning, staring at the illustration of Madame Cheng paper-clipped to the front. There's a bitterness in the back of his throat like ash.

His mother is silence, Madame Cheng a stranger.

Leaving the office, he slips out the back door, down to the beach.

————————

The boy's shadow stretches tall and thin across the sand, and his shaggy hair, stiff with dried saltwater from swimming, whips about his head in the ocean breeze, stinging his cheeks.

Teach chases a dragonfly, darting through the dunes while the boy stands at the cave's threshold. He soaks up both the cold of the dark and the heat of the sun, his body the ecotone.

He glances back, heart beating hard enough he feels it in his teeth. But his parents no longer obey the rules; why should he?

At first, he stays near the entrance waiting for Teach to join him while watching the dark ahead and the mouth behind, making sure the tide doesn't rise on him. His shoulders ache, his hands balled into fists at his sides, but it's damp and dark, a balm on his overheated skin, and the longer he stands there, the more he can see.

There's an outcropping just ahead, a darker shadow trailing out from the wall, bifurcating the area. He stumbles forward on the uneven floor, foot sinking into a puddle of water, but he doesn't fall into any pits or get crushed by rockfall.

He knows it's not an outcropping the moment he touches it, its surface uneven but smooth. It may be some kind of wood, the end sticking up in five knobby protrusions like palm spines without their leaves. Following it toward the wall, the boy encounters cloth, wet and sandy. He jerks his hand back, rubbing it against his shorts.

It doesn't take long to figure out he touched bone—the shape at the end a foot, the cloth pants.

Now that he knows what he's looking at, it's easy to see the details. Above the pants, the torso and shoulders rise and end abruptly—headless.

He hears it breathe, fast and loud against the cave walls, and watches the skeleton for movement, but it's his lungs that burn, his head that feels light and floating, and he realizes he hears only himself.

Every pirate movie he's ever seen has a skeleton, and this is the coolest thing he's ever found, even if a quieter, cooler voice whispers that it's wearing pants. That his mother and father wear pants. That he wears pants.

He leans closer, fingering the material. It's dark and stiff, blue or black maybe, like dress pants. The boy leans closer to look at the neck area and notices a shadow inside the ribs, something moving. It has a rhythm—like a heart, withered but still beating. He leans in, peering through the branches of the rib cage. It has spines that oscillate in waves—a sea urchin. Slipping his hand between the curving bone, he brushes the animal, making it shiver. It's perfect, beautiful.

The boy carefully plucks it, feeling it throb in his hand and then up through his chest, and lower, to his belly. Hunger gouges him, saliva flooding his mouth and drooling onto his chin.

Turning it over in his palm, he bites through the underside, crunching through spines, his teeth digging into the cavity inside. Black, brackish water washes down his chin and chest.

Teach runs into him hard and grips the boy's arm in his teeth, shaking it. The boy cries out and jerks away, dropping the urchin as he clutches his arm, tense in anticipation of pain. It takes a moment to realize it doesn't hurt, that there are no wounds in his flesh. But his mouth tastes of decay. Teach snuffles his arm and gives his cheek an apologetic lick.

Just ahead, deeper in the cave, something heavy scrapes against the rock. The dark shifts, a movement felt more than seen. The boy stands quickly, rattling the bones at his feet, and Teach bares his teeth.

He trembles as he waits for another noise, another shift in the air. There's a stench rising through the dark, like piss and rotting seafood, and he's reminded of the time his mother took him to see the seals at La Jolla.

He's caught between rushing deeper into the dark and retreating back into the sun. Keeping his eyes focused ahead, he picks up a stone, hefting it in his hand. It's just a rock, but it fills him with a mad joy. Rocks, after all, can bring down giants.

Teach grabs his shirt, pulling so the neck presses against his throat and stretches off his shoulder.

"That you, Grandpa?"

He waits in the quiet, caught between his dog and whatever looms in front, eyes wide and aching as he tries to see.

"Grandpa?"

Teach pulls him back with insistent jerks, and the boy grips at his shirt, trying to pull it away from the dog, but he can't take his eyes off the void in front of him.

"You asshole." He hurls the words into the dark with the rock and waits, one second, two. The boy holds his breath, but the rock never lands, and nothing ever answers. He throws another, and another, but the darkness remains absolute, and all he can hear is the rush of the blood in his veins.

Eventually, he lets Teach pull him back into the light. He watches the entrance until the sun sits low in the sky and his stomach aches with hunger.

Before heading home, he checks on his buried treasure, but when he digs down deep, he finds only driftwood and beach glass.

———

That night, in his room, the sheets cool against his hot skin and Teach a solid weight by his side, the boy stares up at the Jolly Roger, its skull grinning down at him.

Teach shifts, his tail whacking the boy's knee, a paw digging into the boy's side. He turns carefully, aware of the edge of the bed, and stares across the room at the model ship that sits on his dresser, the shell his grandfather gave him hidden inside.

Teach stretches, the prickly fur on his lower legs scratching the boy's back.

Eventually, the boy gets up and takes down his pirate flag. He takes the shell from his model ship, running his fingers over its smooth exterior, tracing the whorls like his grandfather had done, but it's just a shell. If its chambers hold secrets, they are too small for him to see.

He tucks it back into his ship and then tosses the whole thing into his closet, breaking the sail and splintering the hull.

He finds his mother in the backyard hanging laundry on the line, the breeze ruffling the white and blue sheets. He stops just short of her, keeping the laundry between them. There's a hesitation in her rhythm, a slight faltering when she realizes he's there. He can't hear her breathe, and he can't smell her perfume over the scent of freshly washed clothes; she's nothing more than a silhouette, a faded image on a film reel flickering on a white screen.

His insides twist and coil.

"Mom?"

In the long minutes before she answers, he starts to believe there's nothing else left of her.

"Yes?"

She steps farther down the line, away from the basket so he can see her bare feet, her toenails painted the color of persimmons.

"How long is Grandpa going to stay?"

She smooths a sheet on the line over and over.

"I don't know," she finally answers. "Until he's ready to go, I guess."

Her voice edges high and cheerful—strained.

The boy hesitates and then looks around, but the sun is bright and painful, and he knows his grandfather hides where it's cool and dark.

"I saw him take money from your purse."

The lie sits heavy between them, the air humid and hard to breathe.

Grabbing the sheet, she tries to yank it back, but he grabs it, too, holding it in place. She has the same persimmon nail polish on her fingernails, chipped and peeling.

His mother smacks his hand and jerks the sheet back. He's left staring at the white flowers on her red dress like blood and bone. He can't make himself look up, and he can't picture her face, just the shape of the wire holding her together.

She grabs his shoulders, fingers digging into their new width, and shakes him. "Where's Teach?"

The fear in her voice makes him look up. "What?"

Her letting go is violent, making him stumble as she backs away.

Teach pushes through the screen door just then, awake from his nap, and meets his dangling hand with a cold nose and a soft *whuf*.

Boy and mother stand there, breathing the same South Carolina heat, listening to the same gulls caw, but somehow they're no longer the same.

He leaves her standing there, unable to shake the uneasiness between them.

———

The boy wakes in the middle of the night, aching and nauseous, a steady pounding between his ears. His mouth and throat feel dry, his eyes gritty and skin tight. The shadows cavort across his ceiling, and his room spins as he sits up.

In the hallway, he finds his father's book open on the floor, the bathroom door closed, its yellow light shining underneath. He continues downstairs. Teach's nails click on the floor behind him. The boy pauses, studying the shadows on the couch, the rise and fall of his grandfather's chest, trying to discern if the old man's eyes are open.

Hurrying into the kitchen, he snags one of the green oatmeal glasses from the dish drainer—the patterns in the cut glass like road maps for his fingers to follow—and fills it with water from the tap. He drinks, liquid leaking from the corners of his mouth to wet his T-shirt. He fills it again, breathing hard between cupfuls. But while the water wets his mouth and throat, it doesn't ease the pain in his head or the roiling in his belly.

He spots the saltshaker on the cabinet, pushed back with the herb rack now that the kitchen table isn't in use. He pours a handful into his palm, a pile of pure white in the dark around him.

Teach *whufs*, pawing at his hip and leg, and the boy shakes his head.

"Don't look at me."

He closes his eyes and licks the salt from his hand. It burns his tongue, his throat, but then his shoulders relax, tension unknotting in his muscles. Another handful and the nausea fades and he can think again.

He wants to take the saltshaker with him. Instead, he puts it back and climbs up on the counter to get the one above the stove, the kitschy ceramic dolphin his mother hides. He checks that it's filled and then secrets it away in the pocket of his shorts before leaving.

On the stairs, he pauses again, looking toward his grandfather, and then hurries the rest of the way upstairs. In the bedroom, he hides the saltshaker in his closet, inside a pair of tennis shoes that are too small for him. Afterward, he lies in the bed trying to forget the smile on the old man's face.

———

Later, on another night, he leans close to whisper in Teach's ear. He tells him how yesterday after church, Lissa Martin followed him down to the river, how her mouth tasted of chocolate frosting and her hair smelled like coconut. He tells him how slick and foreign her tongue felt in his mouth. How saltwater flooded the back of his throat when the thing inside him rose, and how he felt it tickle the tip of her tongue. He tells him how he knew he could grab it and jerk it from her mouth.

The land, his father says, has a long memory. It buries its secrets deep and only millennia later do people dig them up, study them, and discuss what they mean. It's always with reverence that he hands the boy the arrowheads he finds or shows him the articles about a new discovery of ancient bones—evidence of giants that used to roam the Earth. That's history, he says, and it's beautiful.

The boy wishes he was like the land, that he could bury his secrets down deep, hide them until millennia later when what is sharp and dangerous about him could be beautiful, too.

———————

It's the end of summer when the boy and his father go crabbing. They take the skiff out to the inlet, out past cattails and clumps of marsh grass, and sit, each with a hand line, the net by his father's side. Teach lies stretched out in the sun, leg twitching now and again as he dreams.

"You seem really unhappy," his father says.

The boy startles, losing his grip on his line, and has to use his foot to keep it from drowning. He concentrates on getting it back in hand, gulls swooping and crying overhead. He doesn't know what to say. His heart beats hard and his mouth tastes salty and metallic like he's swallowed an old fishing hook. He wonders if this is it, if his father intends to point out the wrongness in him. As sick as the thought makes the boy, he kind of hopes he does. It would be a relief for someone to know.

"Your mom told me you lied about your grandfather the other day."

The boy doesn't say anything. What could he? He's only sorry it didn't work.

"I think you and I, we have similar opinions of him."

There's a tug on the boy's line. His father grabs the net, holding it ready, scooting closer in case the boy should fumble.

Teach snorts, sitting up quickly, sneezing.

"There are two kinds of family," his father says. "The kind you share genes with, and the kind you welcome into your heart." He scoops up the crab and plops it into the bucket. "Sometimes a person can be both, like you and I, but just because you're related to someone doesn't mean you have to keep them in your life."

The boy focuses on the faint hum of traffic on the interstate and tries to think of something to say. The water in the inlet is so calm he imagines sinking to the bottom and letting the sand cover him.

His parents told him his body would change, his interests would change, but no one told him his secrets would change.

They sit for a while longer, waiting, but the sun is well past its zenith, and he knows they're going to have to head home soon.

Teach lays his head in his lap, steadying him—the language they use has changed, but they still understand each other.

"You know I'm proud of you, right?"

The boy shrugs.

"I'm going to tell him he has to leave," his father says. "Things'll get back to normal."

The boy wonders—some changes are permanent—but as they get the skiff on the trailer and load their catch in the back, he starts to relax. Things will never go back to the way they were before, but maybe they can get better.

For the first time in a month, he can see the sun instead of the shadows it creates.

———

That evening, over cracked crab shell and newspaper, his father lays down his edict, and after the raised voices and his mother's silence—her grip white-knuckled on the counter—his father goes for a run and doesn't come back.

The boy watches from his bedroom window, pressing his cheek into the warm wire of the screen. The night is bright and full of noise, spring peepers and owls, and every sort of thing that creeps and crawls out of the lowland swamps at night. Bugs circle the light out by the drive, bats darting and swooping, appearing without warning to snatch them in the middle of flight.

Ten.

How many times has his father told him it's best not to run at night? Too easy to get hit.

Eleven.

His mother stands by the window, unmoving.

Midnight.

The boy calls the police.

They come to the house, but it's not like on TV. There are no flashing lights, no sirens. There's no manhunt through the woods with dogs braying at clues. The only urgency is in the boy's own chaotic heart.

He stands in the porch light, listening to the high whine of cicadas and the distant rush of the ocean as his mother answers the officers' questions.

When he sees someone walking up the drive through the dark, his heart lurches, his anxiety peeling away, leaving him weak and shaky. But Teach stiffens at his side, muzzle wrinkled, a growl trickling past his teeth, and he knows it's not his father.

When his mother sees her father, her face crumples into realization... and then grief. The boy wants to punch the old man. He wants to pull him apart and sink him deep into the marsh.

But the thing is, the boy sort of wants to hit his mother too.

His grandfather rests his hands on her shoulders, and she goes quiet. The old man answers the officer's questions as if he's been there all along.

Rage crashes through the boy. He comes off the steps

quick and hard, with just enough presence of mind to aim himself at his grandfather.

His mother is quicker, though; he doesn't even have time to acknowledge that she's moving before he feels the sting of her palm on his cheek and smells the citrus of her perfume like afterburn.

One officer catches his mother around the waist, pulling her back. Teach lunges, teeth snapping, lip peeled back. The other officer draws his gun and points it at Teach, and then, when the boy grabs Teach's collar, the gun swings back to him—its black hole ugly and infinite. For one breathless moment they stare at each other. The cop, he realizes, doesn't see the monster inside him, doesn't see him at all.

His mother screams something unintelligible, twisting in the other cop's arms.

Again, he wills the thing inside him up.

His grandfather steps between him and the gun, and his mother covers her face with her hands and folds at the waist, her shoulders shaking. Teach presses into his side, body still taut and trembling.

"Tensions are running high," the other officer says.

The old man looks back at the boy, brow wrinkled, unhappy.

The cop lowers his gun and slowly holsters it.

The cops shake hands with the old man before leaving,

and the boy locks gazes with his grandfather. The old man doesn't have to say anything, the boy knows what he's thinking.

Loyalty.

―――――――

His mother withdraws, locking herself behind her blank eyes. She lies in bed curled on her side, covers pulled high even though it's still warm. The boy and Teach keep watch in his parents' bedroom. There's an indentation on his father's side of the bed that hits the boy in the wrong places and hurts in all kinds of ways, but it's safer than what's out in the hall.

Outside the bedroom, there are noises—thumps, clicking, and squelching. Something, some *thing*, leans against the door, rattling it, making it creak and shudder, but the grandfather, he stays outside.

It feels like a taunt, like the bump of a shark's nose before the bite.

By the second night, his empty stomach aches and Teach lies listless at the foot of the bed. His mother is still locked away. The boy lies beside her, watching the window. The moon hangs over the forest, laying down a trail of light against the black treetops, a bright and shining road. He remembers believing he might run down it one day when gravity could no longer hold him back.

He closes his eyes and listens to echoes of past summers.

Mom, be Anne Bonny.

Dad, be Calico Jack.

And they were all pirates together.

———————

On the third night, his mother wakes. Not empty-eyed and loose, but aware, seeing him, seeing Teach. She slips her cold fingers between his. She still won't look him in the eye, but when he squeezes her hand, she squeezes back. She pets Teach, scratching at his ears in a way the boy didn't know she knew. Teach wags his tail, beating the bed with it.

"You're a good kid," she says.

And suddenly he can't look at her. He holds on to Teach and stares at the dusty chest of drawers, at the yellow-tinged light seeping beneath the door as his grandfather passes by, at the window. He waits for an *and* or a *but*, but it never comes.

"I've changed," he says.

She squeezes his hand. "But only in good ways. You're not like him."

"Who?" he asks.

"You're so much like your father."

Her voice breaks on the last word, and he feels it rise, roiling and curling in his belly, pressing up against his ribs like he might crack open with it.

Outside the door, there's a wet thump, but the boy doesn't even bother to look anymore.

"I'm going to kill him," he says.

She goes quiet, still. He turns from her, watching moths crawl across the window screen, their triangular shape like the arrowheads his father used to find. All those tribes—the Pee Dee, Santee, Coosawhatchie, Wateree—all thriving peoples, now reduced to rivers, running, always running.

He waits, expecting her to recoil, to say he's a monster. Instead, she pulls him closer, tugging him down into the bed, into her arms.

"Lie down with me," she says.

He doesn't understand why she won't say it when they both know the truth about what he is.

"Who were you and Dad talking about that day? Who changed?"

She studies his face, his eyes, brushing her thumb over the cheek she'd smacked the night his father disappeared. "Later," she says.

It feels like forever since he's been hugged, but he tells himself he stays in her arms because he's tired. He breathes her in, everything from the acridity of her sweat to her sour breath, the weight of her arms around him soothing.

She runs her fingers through his hair, saying, "Rest. I'm here," and begins telling him a story. Not a pirate story or a sea monster story, but a story about a young woman who ran away to college and the biology student she met there. A handsome boy with bright, intelligent eyes and a cleft chin, a boy who loved to dance and taught her kindness. It's not the story he wants to hear, but he thinks maybe it's the one she needs to tell.

IV

They're woken by his mother's angry shout from the hall, the crack of flesh against flesh.

"Don't you fucking touch him," she says.

Teach jumps from the bed and attacks the door, digging at the wood, barking. The boy's foot catches in the sheet, tripping him, and he hits the floor hard. His mouth fills with blood. Between the throbbing in his face and Teach's fury, he loses what is said.

A thump jars the wall.

By the time he gets free and opens the door, the hallway is empty. He doesn't know what to expect—slime, water, rot and ruin—but it's just a hallway. The only difference is an indentation the size of his hand in the wall, the plaster cracked. It's a small thing, like a period—full stop.

It takes time to get downstairs and out the door into the dark, to get to the field beyond the house, and his grandfather is already so far ahead. He and Teach pelt down toward the beach, sand burrs pricking his bare feet.

He crests the dunes just in time to see the old man disappear into the cave, his mother slung over his shoulder, her long, dangling arms ending in limp, pale hands. He slips and slides down the sand, almost to the cave when Teach darts in front of him and stops, the boy toppling over him. He gets up, dropping sand from his shoulders and hair, and starts again, but Teach pounces on him, pushing him back down.

"Get off me."

He shoves the dog away, runs into the cave, and stops.

The chamber still feels cold and wet, the constant *plip* of dripping water echoing through the cavern, but it's changed. There's a cold bioluminescence, the walls cyanotype blue, the floor speckled with tide pools—tiny universes glowing green and yellow. Long jellied amoebas furred with thin filaments crawl over crags on backward-articulated pincers. And sea urchins, spines vibrating, fill the area with a high, oscillating hum.

There's a moment when he feels disoriented, like he might fall into one of those tide pools, fall forever into some other place. The light pulses in time with the throbbing in his face, and his vision wavers and ripples as if he's seeing everything through water. The humming resonates inside the boy, echoing deep into spaces he thinks a person shouldn't possess, and a breeze swells out of the dark, carrying the stench of ammonia and rot.

Later, he'll remember how reality ended at the folding

of his mother's body, but it's the loud crack of her spine echoing through the cave that makes the boy look to the left, just quick enough to see her on the ground. It isn't until she's drawn back toward his grandfather's maw that he sees his grandfather. He recognizes the glow from his bedroom, the translucent, jellylike dome, but the rest takes time to understand.

The old man's eyes have sunk into his head, his forehead having gone translucent, swelling forward and growing smoothly down until the old man's nostrils and mouth are all that's left. There are shapes inside his head, brownish-white, fibrous lumps. His eyes two white, bulbous mounds, the pupils and irises gone. Beneath the nostrils, his upper lip arches up and out, the sides unfolding to points like the side apexes of a kite. His chin, throat, and upper chest split and peeled back like petals, the inside velvet of its mouth a bright blue and yellow, its throat purple like a tropical flower. There's no tongue. Only tentacles—long, slender things. Translucent. Individually, they look too fragile to be a threat, but they wrap around each other to form thicker, heavier appendages.

The boy starts forward, toward where his mother still lies between them, but his grandfather's eyeballs suddenly roll down, the irises and pupils pointed at him once again, and he freezes where he stands.

His grandfather continues to drag his mother's body back with hands and tentacles until she starts to disappear into his gullet.

Teach rushes forward, a wild thing of teeth and fur and claw, 130,000 years of ancestors. Millennia of living in packs, of hunting and scouting and protecting, pushing him on. Tentacles whip out, wrapping around his torso, and Teach yelps, high and pained as he's lifted from the floor.

His mother disappears, swallowed.

The boy rushes forward, grasping at the slick tendrils wrapped around Teach, trying to pry them loose. Pain lances up from his palms like fire. Unable to hold on, he doubles over, hands tucked into the safety of his chest. His grandfather rams Teach into the wall, cutting the dog off mid-yelp, the silence heavy with the ringing in the boy's head. Tentacles wrap around the boy's ankle, jerking him to the floor and the pain in his hands diminishes in a burst of throbbing, neon bright behind his eyelids.

Crags dig into his back as his grandfather drags him forward. He twists, each ridge he grabs renewing the fire in his palms.

Teach hits low and fast, snarling as he tears into the tentacles around the boy's foot. The monster screams and then makes a coughing noise, choking as his tentacles retreat. Teach snatches the boy by the shirt, forcing him to his feet as he stumbles out and away from the cave.

Halfway across the field, Teach collapses. The boy grabs him, pulling until he gets his feet beneath him again, and they run.

V

This morning, the sun finds the boy sitting at the base of an oak, his nose clogged, his face tight and itchy. There's a deep ache, separate from the swelling bruises and the red raw flesh of his stung hands and ankle. The boys in his books always have a plan, but all he has is an empty spot left by his father, the crack of his mother's spine, and the body of his best friend.

Teach stopped breathing a while ago. Even though the boy removed the stingers—the nematocysts, his father called them—from Teach's mouth, he couldn't stop the swelling of his tongue. He holds the dog's head in his lap, wrapping his arms around his neck while trying to ignore how slack and heavy he is. He presses his face against Teach's ear, feeling the velvety softness against his nose and catching the fading scent of saltwater and sand mixed with Teach's warm, doggy smell. There's something tight wrapped around his chest, squeezing until it hurts to breathe, his throat aching.

"Father was wrong," he tells him. "Sometimes, being related is all it takes."

Teach is still tangible, a last piece of himself he can still see, even if he can never get it back. Leaving him there hurts, but the boy can't stay.

He makes his way through the field, pausing when he catches movement out of the corner of his eye, a shadow trotting beside him, but when he turns and looks there's nothing there.

In the house, his grandfather's shaving kit still sits on the table, his pillow and blanket still folded on the couch, but the house is quiet. There's no rustle of paper from his father's desk, no humming as his mother makes notes, no clicking of claws on hardwood. He closes his eyes and it's like he's not home at all.

Upstairs, his bedroom looks too small to contain everything from his childhood. The blankets hold on to Teach's russet fur, but the walls are plain—white and smooth, the personality scoured away.

There's no sign of where his Jolly Roger hung, and his model ship is still in pieces somewhere in the closet. He fists his hands at his sides, but in the end he digs it up. Inside the split hull, he finds the shell his grandfather gave him—broken. He resists the urge to try to fit the edges back together. Some changes are permanent, and some things, once broken, cannot be put back together again.

He waits by the window, watching, and when his grandfather comes, he looks as normal as he ever did.

As the boy starts down, he's aware of the vastness inside, a door leading to new places, to new voices. Blood, he remembers his father telling him, is our own red-tinted ocean, and the ocean, he knows, is where life began.

All he has to do is open himself up.

The boy stops on the threshold of the kitchen, staring at the old man, hating his grin and his sea-colored eyes that remind him of his mother.

"It hurts like hell the first time, but anger helps. Come on, boy, I killed your mama. Get angry at me."

The anger is already there, so much that he can't hold it all. He wills it up, out of himself, straining to push his body into a new configuration, but nothing happens.

His grandfather stops smiling. He crosses the room and smacks the boy in the mouth, making it bleed again.

"What's the matter with you? Don't you care about nothing?"

The boy covers his lips with his hand, catching bloody drool. It takes a minute to shove that shock away and then the boy launches at him, no tentacles, just fists and feet. He lands a solid blow to the old man's nose and blood runs from him like chumming the water. The boy swings and kicks and bites; he tries to dig his fingers into the old man's throat and eyes.

The grandfather's grip on him tightens, clamping down on his arm and gripping his hair as he opens swift and easy, his mouth and throat peeling back. His eyes sink into his head. Tentacles loop about the boy's neck and body, prying him off. The sting burns and the tentacles smell sick—like a sinus infection. The boy scrabbles against the slick flesh, his nails sliding off the rubbery strands, mucus under his nails, creating webs between his fingers. The tentacles tighten around his chest, squeezing until there's no room for breath.

The boy struggles, and then he doesn't. He is so tired of feeling scared, of waiting for things to come together so the world feels right again. He goes limp and closes his eyes, waiting for his throat to swell closed, willing to let himself go.

He is ready.

The tentacles aim for his mouth, trying to worm their way between his lips and through his clenched teeth. The boy arches his neck and turns his head away. The old man twists him until it hurts so much he has to scream. The tentacles slip into his mouth and across his tongue, and his world disappears in black spots that spread like ink.

———————

The boy wakes, aching. Automatically, he reaches for the warmth of fur at his side, but there's only linoleum and the pain in his throat and face. He runs his fingers over his mouth and chin, down his neck, setting the stings on fire.

There is a seam dividing him, a mark of before and after.

Outside, a car door closes. He stands, stumbling, his body heavy and awkward around him.

The grandfather's belongings are gone from the table, the pillow and blanket from the couch. He exits out the back door, pausing at the empty pants and empty shirts still hanging on the line like flags, his yellow-and-black T-shirt on the end swaying in the breeze—danger.

Around the house, he pauses in the shadow, watching as the old man comes around and up to the porch, through the front door.

His grandfather is right; it hurts when he pries himself open, letting himself writhe into the open air for the first time like a gasping breath. His vision goes watery again, spinning like a gyroscope, the eyes inside his head swiveling to look up and then behind. Everything is too bright, washed out until the world loses its edges like an overexposed photograph.

He loses his balance, falling to his knees, hands full of grass and sand as his stomach lurches. Pushing to his feet, he stumbles into a tree, the bark rough against his shoulder, and wishes he could close his eyes. Eventually, he gets his feet beneath him, the world stabilizing enough that he doesn't fall down.

The boy finds his grandfather mostly by sound, the opening of the front door and the crunch of his feet over gravel as he rounds the car. He catches him before he can change and he follows the old man's earlier actions like a template. He whips around him, wrapping his grandfather's jaw and neck tight to keep him from opening, and squeezes.

The old man pulls at the boy's tentacles, those sea-blue eyes wide and panicked, and the monster pauses. The old man is all he has now, his only family. Without him, there's nothing to anchor the boy anywhere. Where will he live? Who will help him when he gets stuck on a math problem? Who will teach him about what came before and what to look for next? Even if he kills the old man, he'll never be free of him; he is, after all, his grandfather.

His grip starts to slacken, and the old man works his fingers beneath his tentacles, loosening them, his chest expanding.

The boy feels the phantom brush of fur against his dangling hand, a solid weight against his leg, and the boy grabs tight, holding on. He remembers his mother's words: *He's my father.*

He looks at the man with his mother's eyes and knows exactly what he's thinking.

Loyalty, boy. You help your family out.

The boy wraps a few tentacles around the old man's

wrist, jerking his hand away, and tightens around his neck, vicious. He rams the old man's head into the side of the station wagon until it's as misshapen as his mother's was. He wants to rage, to stomp and scream.

He remembers, though, the day of the hurricane, the way his mother watched him, how she turned from him. He remembers her story about meeting his father, the feel of her fingers through his hair as she lulled him down to sleep.

The old man's neck cracks and the boy lets go.

———

It turns out folding up is even harder than unfolding. Coils bulge and escape, and when he finally pulls himself together, he feels uneven where he split apart.

He stares at the old man's body, waiting, just to be sure he's dead.

The world is utterly quiet and he's utterly alone.

He sits down on the porch steps, wondering what he's supposed to do next. He wants to know if he's done the right thing, but the longer he sits there, the less sure he becomes.

His ears and nostrils are not slit, but they might as well be.

———

He finds the place where he left Teach, the dirt stained with his friend's blood. But there's no dog, only a large cocoon attached to the tree. He sits down and watches, balling his hands in his lap as he waits.

Days pass.

He drinks from the ocean and eats mulberries, persimmons, and chestnuts from the forest. He avoids the house—that empty shell. He's a wild thing now, and wild things have no domestic home. When he's scared, he goes into the dark, to the cave where he dragged his grandfather's corpse, and watches, just to be sure. And when he's sad, he curls up next to the cocoon and presses his face to the tree. Most of the time, he doesn't feel anything at all except the crack of his grandfather's neck.

Some monsters are real after all.

When the sun is low in the sky, he spends hours on the beach, tucked among the rocks. Sometimes, when he closes his eyes, he hears his mother's voice in the cadence of the waves and he listens to the ebb and flow, the stories they tell, remembering. He can imagine her again, standing proud and defiant as she leads a fleet across the ocean.

And if the waves whisper him stories, then the forest sings him lullabies, melodies passed down through fossil and bone. But he's not the land, and burying things down deep doesn't render them mute.

One morning, as the sun rises, there's movement inside the cocoon. Whatever it is, it's so much larger than Teach ever was.

Maybe, he thinks, everyone's wrapper is small. Maybe we all have doors inside leading to cracked places and wild spaces.

The cocoon begins to rip.

Some events, once lived through, can never be forgotten. And some changes are permanent. But he leans forward anyway, the silk of the cocoon like the brush of fur, and whispers.

Acknowledgments

I would like to express my deepest gratitude to all those who supported me in the creation of this book. To my editor, Ellen Datlow, who said yes to giving the manuscript of a relatively unknown author a read, and then for the hours spent combing and tweaking to polish it. You've made dreams come true.

My thanks also go to the crew at Tordotcom Publishing. To Emily Goldman and Irene Gallo and all those working behind the scenes. Thank you not only for the hard work, but for making this a wonderful experience.

To my friend, mentor, and colleague Richard Thomas. Thank you for believing in me and this story. Your support, encouragement, and guidance have meant the world to me. I wouldn't be here without you and Storyville.

Thank you also to my dear friend and mentor Scott Phillips. You were the first to believe in me. Thank you for your kindness, and for giving me the belief and courage to continue writing when I was so lost.

To all of those who read and commented, thank you. Special thanks go to Pamela Durgin and Kris Majury.

Thank you for reading each and every iteration of this. Your patience is a gift, and so is your friendship.

To Sha'lane Chatenay, thank you for telling me about pirates. Your friendship, enthusiasm, and knowledge are greatly appreciated.

And finally, to my family. Especially to my father, who taught me about the land and the sea, and to my grandmother for passing along her love of stories. I miss you both every day.

About the Author

Christy Oaks of C. Oaks Photography

S. L. CONEY obtained a master's degree in clinical psychology before abandoning academia to pursue a writing career. The author has ties to South Carolina and roots in St. Louis, and is still deeply disappointed their fins never grew in. Coney's work has appeared in *St. Louis Noir, The Best American Mystery Stories 2017,* and *Gamut Magazine.*

TOR·COM

Science fiction. Fantasy. The universe.

And related subjects.

*

More than just a publisher's website, *Tor.com*

is a venue for **original fiction, comics,** and

discussion of the entire field of SF and fantasy,

in all media and from all sources. Visit our site

today—and join the conversation yourself.